Franklin's Nickname

From an episode of the animated TV series *Franklin* produced by
Nelvana Limited, Neurones France s.a.r.l. and Neurones Luxembourg S.A.

Based on the Franklin books by
Paulette Bourgeois and Brenda Clark.

TV tie-in adaptation written by Sharon Jennings
and illustrated by John Lei, Sasha McIntyre and Jelena Sisic.

Based on the TV episode *Franklin's Nickname*, written by Frank Diteljan.

Kids Can Press acknowledges the financial support of the Government of Ontario, through
the Ontario Media Development Corporation's Ontario Book Initiative; the Ontario Arts Council;
the Canada Council for the Arts; and the Government of Canada, through the BPIDP, for our
publishing activity.

Kids Can Press Ltd.
29 Birch Avenue
Toronto, ON M4V 1E2

www.kidscanpress.com

Series editor: Tara Walker
Edited by Yvette Ghione

Printed in China by WKT Company Limited

The hardcover edition of this book is smyth sewn casebound.
The paperback edition of this book is limp sewn with a drawn-on cover.

CM 04 0 9 8 7 6 5 4 3 2 1
CDN PA 04 0 9 8 7 6 5 4 3 2 1

National Library of Canada Cataloguing in Publication Data

Jennings, Sharon
        Franklin's nickname / Sharon Jennings ; illustrated by John Lei,
Sasha McIntyre, Jelena Sisic.

(A Franklin TV storybook.)
The character Franklin was created by Paulette Bourgeois and Brenda Clark.
ISBN 1-55337-489-4 (bound).   ISBN 1-55337-490-8 (pbk.).

I. Lei, John II. McIntyre, Sasha III. Sisic, Jelena IV. Bourgeois, Paulette
V. Clark, Brenda VI. Title. VII. Series: Franklin TV storybook.

PS8569.E563F745 2003   jC813'.54   C2003-904252-9

Kids Can Press is a ʟ℮ʀᴜs™ Entertainment company

Franklin's Nickname

Kids Can Press

FRANKLIN could score goals in hockey and hit home runs in baseball. He could dribble a basketball and kick a soccer ball. Franklin wanted to be a famous athlete when he grew up. Then one day, Mr. Owl asked his students to do projects on sports heroes. That's when Franklin discovered he had a problem.

Franklin chose his favorite soccer player, "Bounce" Baboon. First, he spent lots of time in the library looking for information. Then he searched for photos in newspapers and magazines.

Soon, the classroom was decorated with everyone's reports.

Franklin looked at all the other projects. He read out the names of the athletes.

There was Slugger and Slider and King. There was Lightning and Giant and Blaze.

"Every athlete has a nickname," Franklin said.

Then he thought for a moment.

"If I'm going to be a famous athlete, I'd better get a nickname, too," he said.

Franklin spent the rest of the afternoon thinking about nicknames. Maybe he could be called Rocket. Or Comet. Or maybe Flash. Franklin smiled. Franklin the Flash. That sounded good.

"Earth to Franklin," called Beaver. "School's over."

Franklin jumped up and ran after his friends.

On the school bus, Franklin let everyone
know that he had picked a nickname.

"From now on, call me Flash," he announced.

"You can't just give yourself a nickname,"
said Beaver. "Others get to decide."

"Because of something you do," added Bear.

"And you're definitely *not* Flash," said Beaver.

Franklin frowned.

Beaver thought for a few moments.

"I know!" she exclaimed. "We'll call you Pokey!"

"Pokey's no good!" Franklin declared.

"How can I be a famous athlete if I'm called Pokey?"

"It suits you, Franklin," replied Bear. "We're always telling you to hurry up."

"It's cute," added Beaver.

Franklin scowled.

At home, Franklin asked everyone to call
him Flash. His mother forgot and called him Honey.
His father forgot and called him Buddy.

His little sister, Harriet, remembered, but she
called him something that sounded like Fwass.
Franklin went to his room to think.

The next day was Saturday, and Franklin had a plan. He hurried to meet his friends at the park.

"Hey, Pokey!" called Beaver. "We've been waiting for you."

Franklin smiled.

"After today, you won't be calling me Pokey anymore," he said.

Everyone was curious.

"I will prove that I'm Franklin the Flash," Franklin said.

"How?" asked Bear.

Franklin pointed to his bike.

"I'll ride my bike around the park three times in a flash," he announced.

"Good idea," said Bear. And he jumped on his bike, too.

Franklin pedaled as fast as he could. But on the second time around, he got slower and slower. His front wheel began to wobble, and Franklin fell over.

Bear kept going.

"Come on, Franklin!" he cried. "Don't stop now!"

Franklin groaned and didn't move.

In a little while, Franklin had another plan.

"I'll swim to the other side of the pond in a flash," he said.

"Good idea," said Beaver.

Franklin jumped into the water. So did Beaver.

When Franklin reached the other side, Beaver was already there.

"Give up?" she asked.

"Never," said Franklin.

Franklin thought and thought.

"I will run up the hill in a flash," he finally said.

"Good idea," said Rabbit.

Halfway up, Franklin huffed and puffed and came to a stop. Rabbit ran by him all the way to the top.

"Keep going, Franklin!" cried Rabbit. "You're almost there!"

Franklin sighed and sat down.

His friends sat down beside him.

"Do you want to try something else?" asked Beaver.

"Maybe tomorrow," replied Franklin. "Right now, I'm too tired."

"And I'm hungry," added Bear.

Everyone else was hungry, too.

Franklin jumped up.

"I have ice-cream bars at home!" he said. "Wait here and I'll be back in a flash!"

Everyone waited as Franklin ran down the hill and across the meadow. They waited as he hurried over the bridge and through the berry patch. They waited as Franklin reached home and asked his mother for ice-cream bars.

They waited as Franklin hunted through the
icebox. They waited as he ran through the berry
patch, over the bridge and across the meadow.
Then they got tired of waiting and left.

Franklin ran back up the hill and looked
for his friends. Then he looked at the ice-cream
bars melting in his hands.

"Hmmm," said Franklin. "I have lots of
time to grow up and become a famous athlete.
I have lots of time to get a really good nickname.
But there sure isn't lots of time for these
ice-cream bars."

And in a flash, Franklin ate them all.